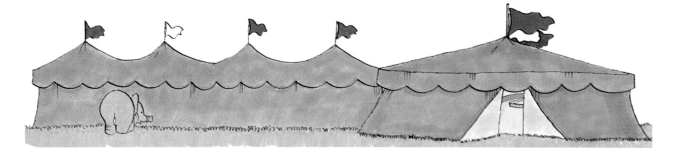

Paulie & Sasha
Circus or Not

AUTHOR'S NOTE

The mission of Paulie and Sasha is to encourage children to be good citizens; to respect the differences of others; to appreciate and respect their own differences; to cultivate a multicultural, cross-cultural understanding; and to respect the earth and community.

For Dave, whose support has made this dream a reality

First printing

PUBLISHED BY DINGLES & COMPANY
P.O. Box 508, Sea Girt, New Jersey 08750
WEBSITE: www.dingles.com • E-MAIL: info@dingles.com

Library binding edition distributed by **GUMDROP BOOKS™**
P.O. Box 505, Bethany, M.O. 64424 • Phone (660) 425-7777
WEBSITE: www.gumdropbooks.com • E-MAIL: wecare@gumdropbooks.com

Library of Congress Cataloging-in-Publication Data
Zocchi, Judy Mazzeo
Series: Paulie and Sasha
Title: Circus or Not
Summary: When Paulie's circus audition goes wrong, it looks like his big top dreams won't ever come true.
Now this spirited bear from New Jersey is chasing new adventures with Sasha,
a circus bear from a far-off land with big dreams of his own.

Library of Congress Catalog Card Number: 98-092883
ISBN 1-891997-17-3

Printed in the U.S.A.

Editors: Pamela Pollack & Andrea Curley Book Design: Rachel Simon
Thanks to: Barbie Lambert, Danielle Austen, Cindy Hart, Tricia Zocchi, Vincent and Rosemary Mazzeo,
and Transworld Management Services, Inc.

Paulie & Sasha
Circus or Not

BY JUDY ZOCCHI

ILLUSTRATED BY DON VANNOZZI

dingles & company

new jersey

Ever since he was a cub growing up in New Jersey,
Paulie dreamed of being a circus bear. Now the Red White and Blue Circus was holding a big tryout. It was the day Paulie had been waiting for all his life.

Paulie was surprised at how many bears were at the audition. "Wow! I never saw so many wannabe circus bears in my life," he said to the bearded lady, who pinned the number 85 on him.

The clown with the clipboard was trying to keep the line moving. "Next," he said briskly.

Bear Number 81 stepped forward and put his arms above his head. In one swift movement, he performed six perfect back flips.

The ringmaster nodded. "Bear Number 81 to the costume tent," the clown with the clipboard announced. "Next."

As Paulie and the other bears watched, Bear Number 82 started to juggle three eggs. The ringmaster shook his head, NO!

"Next," the clown with the clipboard shouted. Startled, Bear Number 82 juggled the eggs onto his head and walked away with yolks dripping all over him.

"Whoa, that ringmaster's tough," Paulie said to Bear Number 86. "That poor bear."

When Paulie's turn came, he thought about how long he had waited for this moment.

"Good luck, 85," Bear Number 86 said.

Paulie approached the big top. His face felt hot, his paws started to sweat, and his stomach felt like a bottomless pit.

He bowed his head, spread out his arms, and started his somersaults. His first roll was perfect; but as he picked up speed, he rolled into the ringmaster, knocked him to the ground, and rolled right over him.

"Next," the clown with the clipboard shouted.

Paulie was very sad when the circus turned him away. His dream had not come true. He wandered around for hours wondering what to do next. He didn't realize how late it was getting, or that it was starting to get dark. Paulie looked around and realized he was at the docks. Ships were getting ready to sail all over the world.

Paulie saw a shipping trailer filled with red tomatoes. He took one and bit into it. "Wow! Jersey tomatoes!"

Paulie walked inside the trailer. It looked like a good place to take a nap. Within minutes, he was asleep.

Not noticing Paulie, a dock worker closed the door of the trailer and locked it.

As he pushed the bar across the back of the door, he sang the dock worker's song:

> *One comes in,*
> *One comes out.*
> *Cross the country,*
> *Ship it out!*

Then a crane lifted the trailer and loaded it onto a ship. The ship's captain rang the horn and sang the ship captain's song:

> *Take it where it's gotta go,*
> *Brave through sleet and hail*
> *and snow.*
> *Sail the sea, day and night,*
> *Till you spot the land in sight!*

The captain sailed the ship to a faraway shore, where another crane lifted the trailer off the ship and loaded it onto a train.

The train's engineer blew the whistle and sang the train engineer's song:

Take it down the beaten track,
Pull it front and push it back.
Pass it to the nearest truck—

And the truck drivers answered, as they loaded the trailer: "Don't look now, the wheels are stuck." The wheels were spinning and splashing mud in every direction.

The truck dispatcher shouted:

Heave ho, let's go.
Bring this to the river barge,
Hope this trailer's not too large.

Finally, the truck drivers unloaded the trailer from the truck onto a barge that was about to sail down the Moscow River. They watched the barge float quietly out of sight.

After several hours of floating down the river, the barge suddenly came to a stop. The trailer was lifted off the barge and the doors were unlocked.

"Ah, fresh air!" Paulie said, swinging the doors open. Leaving the trailer when no one was looking, he stretched his arms, took a long sniff, and looked around the docks. He had no idea where he was. There was a red white and blue flag flying on the flagpole. But it wasn't the American flag.

"Wow!" Paulie said. "I don't believe this." He heard a song playing on the radio. But it wasn't in English. "Where am I?" he shouted to a bear carrying a stick with a pouch at the end of it.

"You are at the port in Murmansk, Russia," the bear answered. Paulie was surprised to see that the bear was dressed in an outfit like his.

"Is that a circus suit?" Paulie asked.

"*Da*," the bear answered.

"*Da?*" Paulie was puzzled. "Are you looking for your father?"

The bear shook his head.

"Da da da dum....da da da dum...." Paulie hummed the tune of the wedding march. "I know. You're getting married."

"I certainly am not," the bear replied. "In Russian '*da*' means 'yes'."

Paulie still looked bewildered. "I forgot the question," he admitted.

"I answer yes," the bear explained. "I am wearing a circus suit. You see, always, since I was a cub, I have wanted to be in the Moscow Circus. Today I try out and they say *nyet*."

Now Paulie was really confused. "'*Nyet*'? What is '*nyet*'?"

"In Russian '*nyet*' means 'no'." Sasha hung his head low.

Paulie said,"I know that *nyet*. I tried out for the Red White and Blue Circus in America and they said no. I mean *nyet*."

"So you are sad?"

Paulie hung his head.

Sasha stood up straight and proud. "If the Moscow Circus doesn't want me, I will sail away and find a circus that does."

Paulie reached into his pocket. "Well, ya gotta eat something first." He handed him a tomato. "What's your name?"

"Sasha," the bear said.

"Mine is Paulie. Paulie from New Jersey. And this, my friend, is a Jersey tomato."

Sasha bit into the tomato, squirting juice in Paulie's eyes. "I am so sorry, Paulie from...?"

Wiping his eyes, Paulie said, "From New Jersey, which is conveniently located on the eastern shore of the United States of America." Paulie picked up three tomatoes and started to juggle them.

"Wow!" Sasha said. "In my country we only juggle balls, fire, and swords."

All of a sudden, Sasha did eight perfect flips in a row. "I flip," he said.

"With flips like that, why didn't you get into the circus?" Paulie asked.

"I was afraid to climb the high pole and walk the high wire," Sasha said.

"Don't sweat it. Everyone's afraid of something," said Paulie.

"I am not sweating," said Sasha.

"In America, 'don't sweat it' means 'don't worry,'" Paulie explained.

"Double meanings? Two meanings is too many." Sasha shook his head. "Are you afraid of anything, Paulie from New Jersey?"

"I'm afraid if we don't get moving, we won't get a ride out of here."

Sasha picked up his pouch and looked inside. "I almost forgot my port pass."

"What's a port pass?" Paulie asked. "It is a little book you have to show to travel from one country to another," said Sasha.

"Oh, you mean a passport. I don't have one. I got locked inside that trailer by accident and ended up here," Paulie said. "We'll have to sneak onto one of the boats."

"What about that one there?" Sasha pointed to a cruise ship. Paulie and Sasha crawled up the ramp.

"Jump on the ledge and pull yourself onto the poop deck," Paulie said.

"'Poop deck'. Is this another double meaning?"

"No," Paulie said. "Just jump."

"I think we're safe," Paulie whispered when they had both landed on the boat deck. "Try to be quiet."

"I hope you are right," Sasha said, stepping on Paulie's toes.

"Eeowww!" yelled Paulie, just as the ship's captain was walking by.

"You. Both of you. Come here immediately," said the captain in a stern voice.

Paulie and Sasha looked at the captain, looked at each other, and took off across the deck. The captain and crew chased them to the rear of the boat.

"Oh no," Sasha yelled. "There is no place to go."

"Oh yes, there is," Paulie answered, "up." He pointed to a high pole.
"Up and then across the cable."

"Up," Sasha repeated with a lump in his throat. The captain and crew were gaining on them. Without even thinking that he didn't like high poles, Sasha shimmied up and ran across not one, not two, but three cables to the other side of the ship.

"Wow. Look at him go," Paulie said to someone behind him. It was the cruise ship captain. "Oh no," Paulie said, shimmying up the pole and across the cable after Sasha.

Paulie and Sasha leaped off the deck of the cruise ship and tumbled onto a barge pulling out of port. The barge was carrying shipping trailers. Paulie and Sasha climbed into a trailer and closed the doors behind them, locking themselves inside.

"I don't believe it," Paulie said, feeling something squish beneath him. "Jersey tomatoes."

"Quite a few of them," Sasha agreed.

"The way you climbed that pole, I bet you could get into the Moscow Circus now," Paulie told Sasha.

"I do not want to, Paulie from New Jersey," said Sasha. "I want to travel with you and find a circus together."

Sasha gave Paulie a bear hug. "Friend," he said.

"Friend," said Paulie. "I can't believe I'm in a trailer on a boat again—the same one, I think. I wonder where it's going now?"

"We will find out soon, I am sure," Sasha said. "Let us make up a song and sing it while we travel."

So Paulie and Sasha ate tomatoes and sang the song they made up while the barge carried them somewhere across the ocean...but where?

CIRCUS OR NOT

HERE WE COME

WITH A PILE OF TOMATOES

YUM...YUM...YUM

WE TRAVELED HERE

WE TRAVELED THERE

NOT SO BAD

FOR A COUPLE OF BEARS

WE BOTH HAVE EARS

WE BOTH HAVE A SNOUT

WE EAT WHEN WE'RE HUNGRY

WE SING AND WE SHOUT

AS THE TRIP WENT ON

WE LEARNED TO BE FRIENDS

WE SANG AND DANCED

UNTIL THE EVENING'S END

MEET THOM FROM NEW JERSEY AND HELEN FROM RUSSIA

Thom Salawy, Age 9
NEW JERSEY, THE UNITED STATES OF AMERICA

Helen Skhirtlaoz, Age 12
SOCHI, RUSSIA

WHERE I LIVE...I live in a small town in New Jersey, near the Atlantic Ocean. I know almost everyone.

ABOUT MY FAMILY...My family is my dad, my mom, my sister, Libby, and me— and I'm going to have a new sister or brother soon. I have a pet frog named Jim, Sr.

THINGS I LIKE TO DO...play video games, ride my bike and skateboard, play basketball with my friends, write stories, draw, and sing.

WHAT I LIKE ABOUT MYSELF...I can run fast. I have a lot of friends. The birthmark on my back. And that I have a caring family.

WHEN I TRY OUT FOR SOMETHING...I feel unsure of myself but I always believe I have a chance.

IF I MAKE IT...It's the best feeling in the world: proud of myself, excited, and happy.

IF I DON'T MAKE IT...I feel sad and disappointed. It's the worst feeling. Sometimes I even feel like crying.

TO FEEL BETTER...I talk to someone else who didn't make it. I talk to my parents. I tell myself a lot of other people didn't make it either.

WHAT ADVICE WOULD YOU GIVE PAULIE AND SASHA?...Never give up trying to reach your goal.

WHERE I LIVE...I live in Sochi, a town on the sea. It is always warm. There are a lot of trees and not a lot of buildings. My favorite thing is the gallery that sells everything—I like to go in-line skating there.

ABOUT MY FAMILY...My mother, dad, 22-year-old brother and his girlfriend (she is like a sister to me), and my grandma live in my house. My uncle has an apartment nearby. His wife just had a baby. When we have birthday parties, they last for 24 hours; and when there is something to celebrate, the whole city has a big party. I have 2 cats, 2 dogs, and 2 parrots.

THINGS I LIKE TO DO...sing, dance, act, play piano, ice skate, and in-line skate.

WHAT I LIKE ABOUT MYSELF...everything. I'm very lazy, but I like that too.

WHEN I TRY OUT FOR SOMETHING AND DON'T MAKE IT...I feel so bad, like nobody likes me and I don't have any talent.

TO FEEL BETTER...I relax and watch television. I call my friends and stay on the phone for hours. I tell them everything that happened. My friends are so caring.

WHAT ADVICE WOULD YOU GIVE PAULIE AND SASHA?...Even if you work hard, work harder- don't put stress on yourself, and never give up.

WHAT DO YOU THINK???

What do Paulie and Sasha have in common? • What are the differences between Paulie and Sasha? • The colors in the American flag and the Russian flag are the same. What are they? • Do you think Paulie and Sasha would make a good circus team?

WHAT ADVICE WOULD YOU GIVE???

When they tried out for the circus, Paulie and Sasha were turned away. What advice would you give them? • How do you feel if you try out for something and don't make it? • What advice would you give to a friend in the same situation? • What do you do to help yourself feel better?

TRY SOMETHING NEW...

Circus bears Paulie and Sasha decided to team up and travel the world together. You could team up with somebody at school. Pick a person you don't know well to work on a project, play a game, or eat lunch together. Then write to Paulie and Sasha and tell them: What did you learn about the new person? What did you like best about him or her? What did you have in common?

Bonus Question: How many Z's are in the author's and illustrator's names?

Answer the questions above and send your answers to Paulie and Sasha. Use a separate piece of paper, and don't forget your name and address.

Mail your answers to:
Paulie & Sasha
dingles & company
P.O. Box 508, Sea Girt, N.J. 08750
Or E-mail Paulie & Sasha @ dingles.com

WHERE IN THE WORLD WILL PAULIE AND SASHA GO NEXT?

Can you figure out where Paulie and Sasha are going next?
Here are some clues.

It's on the Atlantic Ocean.

It's on the same continent as Kenya.

The capital of the country is Brazzaville.

This is the flag of the country.

See if you guessed right when the next Paulie and Sasha adventure, THE RESCUE, arrives in your local bookstore. Coming soon...

Visit our Website at http:// www.dingles.com